MR PANCAKE

Stephanie Baudet

Sweet Cherry
Publishing

Published by Sweet Cherry Publishing Limited
Unit 36, Vulcan House
Vulcan Road
Leicester, LE5 3EF
United Kingdom

First published in the UK in 2013
This edition published 2017
ISBN: 978-1-78226-243-5
©Stephanie Baudet 2013
Illustrations ©Creative Books
Illustrated by Ojoswi Sur & Joy Das

Mr Pattacake and the Big Idea

Lexile® code numerical measure L = Lexile® 810L

Wai Man Book Binding (China) Ltd. Kowloon, H.K.

Pattacake, Pattacake, baker's man,
Bake me a cake as fast as you can;
Pat it and prick it and mark it with P,
Put it in the oven for you and for me.

Pattacake, Pattacake, baker's man,
Bake me a cake as fast as you can;
Roll it up, roll it up;
And throw it in a pan!

Pattacake, Pattacake, baker's man.

MR PATTACAKE
and the
BIG IDEA

Mr Pattacake picked up the envelope off the mat and opened it, peering closely at the writing. His eyes widened and he smiled a big smile.

'Yippee!' he shouted.

He then did a silly little dance on the spot. Now, it's not a good idea to do silly dances when holding a mug of tea, and it spilt over the side and slopped over the letter.

'**Oh DRIBBLE !**' said Mr Pattacake. He
always said that when he was cross.

His big chef's hat wobbled as he shook the drops
of tea off the letter.

'Look at this, Treacle,' he said, showing the letter to his cat, who had nearly jumped out of his skin when Mr Pattacake had shouted.

'I'm in business! I've been asked to make the food for a children's birthday party,' said Mr Pattacake. 'There will be one hundred children!' He waved the letter in the air.

Treacle didn't answer. He was only a cat after all. He did what all cats do. He just went on washing his paw as if he had not heard... But he knew what Mr Pattacake had said. Being in business meant being busy, and in Mr Pattacake's case, that meant busy cooking and baking. Treacle knew there was always something for him to eat when Mr Pattacake was cooking, which was why he had grown into such a big, fat cat.

'I must start planning,' said Mr Pattacake. 'Such a lot of food to make.' He threw the letter onto the worktop where it slowly soaked up a puddle of spilt ketchup.

He then put on his glasses and sat at the table making a list of what he would need. He had to make sure that this was the best party ever for… what was his name? He picked up the letter and wiped off the ketchup with his sleeve so he could read the name. It was for Jack. It was his eighth birthday.

Treacle sat looking up at Mr Pattacake, his ears pricked up, listening intently.

'Right,' said Mr Pattacake. 'We'll make pizzas and monkey tail sandwiches. And we'll have popcorn and crisps and fruit kebabs. And sausages on sticks too.'

Treacle stared hard at Mr Pattacake.

'Oh, of course, Treacle. There are the chocolate mice. I hadn't forgotten.' Mr Pattacake was famous for his chocolate mice.

Treacle seemed to nod slightly.

'So, we'll need…' Mr Pattacake bent over the piece of paper to write.

Ten loaves of bread,

A kilo of chicken,

A thousand mini sausages,

Fruit,

Cream cheese and sultanas,

Lots of drinks and crisps,

Popping corn,

Chocolate for the chocolate mice,

And jelly. Lots and lots of jelly. Children loved jelly and ice cream.

And then there was the special cake. That was the thing that Mr Pattacake loved doing most. He always tried to make the cake as realistic as possible. This one would need wheels, and so he was going to use *real* ones.

At last the list was finished. Mr Pattacake loved making lists. It was an important part of planning, he always said, and the planning was just as important as the cooking.

Sometimes he even made lists when there *wasn't* a cooking job. There were lists of food that he liked, lists of songs that he whistled whilst he was cooking, and one day, he had even made a list of naughty things that Treacle did – which was the longest list of all! Like when he stayed out playing all night, and when he stole some little sausages Mr Pattacake had just cooked, and hid them under his bed.

On the day of the party Mr Pattacake got up very early and jumped in his little yellow van to buy the food.

There was a lot of it, and he staggered indoors with heavy bags and boxes.

Soon the big fridge in his kitchen was full. A dozen boxes were stacked on the floor and several bulging bags were on the worktops. Some contained fruit – apples, oranges, strawberries and bananas. Then there were boxes of crisps, and sliced bread. Treacle sat on top of a stack of boxes containing the chocolate. He knew what Mr Pattacake would be making first.

The chocolate mice.

And chocolate mice were the next best thing to real mice.

Mr Pattacake got out his biggest pan to melt the chocolate. Soon it was glop-glopping and spitting out little showers of chocolate onto the floor and the worktop.

Treacle was not allowed on the worktop but he *was* allowed on the floor. He licked up the drops of chocolate as they rained down on him, darting from place to place as a new drop fell. Then he sat and washed his whiskers, purring contentedly.

Mr Pattacake poured the chocolate into the mouse moulds and found a space on the worktop for them to set. He put in little silver balls for eyes and stuck a piece of edible string to each one for a tail. One of the tails was a little longer than the rest and hung down over the edge of the worktop.

Later on, when Mr Pattacake was not looking, that particular little mouse escaped. The chef didn't notice. He was busy spreading the slices of bread with two delicious fillings. There was chicken and avocado, and there was cream cheese, carrot and sultanas. He then rolled them up and cut them into round monkey tail sandwiches. He boiled the big kettle to make the jelly, and greased the trays to cook the sausages.

The kitchen was full of steam and he could barely see, so he had to take off his glasses, wipe them with his handkerchief and switch off the kettle. Then he bent down to get his big jelly moulds out of the cupboard. But as he reached out, he clumsily knocked the tray of chocolate mice with his elbow. They all flew into the air, tails waving and silver eyes sparkling.

They tumbled back down, with some landing on the floor and some on the worktop. A few had ears missing and some were smashed into a hundred pieces.

'**Oh DRIBBLE !**' Mr Pattacake sighed. He picked up the mice he could salvage from the ones which had landed on the worktop, pulled off their tails, and popped them back into the pan to melt. He would have to start all over again, but Mr Pattacake was used to things going wrong.

Treacle had watched the mice flying through the air, especially the ones that had flown off the worktop. He had been a very good cat and cleaned the floor up. Not one bit of the chocolate mice was left. He licked his lips and lay on the floor, his tummy full.

Suddenly, Treacle's ears twitched, and he looked towards the window. A dark furry face was peering in.

Treacle was used to children sometimes looking in to see what Mr Pattacake was cooking. Mr Pattacake would always take off his hat and wave it at them, giving them each a piece of a broken chocolate mouse. (The mice were very accident-prone.)

But *children* did not have furry faces. Treacle's fur stood on end and he made a horrible yowling noise.

'Be quiet, Treacle. I'm trying to think,' said the chef. But Treacle jumped onto the worktop (where he was not allowed) and stared out of the window, nose to nose with the black furry face outside. It was lucky that there was a pane of glass between them; he might not have been so brave had it not been there. Tortoiseshell cats could be very fierce, you see.

He yowled again, and this time Mr Pattacake looked up. 'Who is it, Treacle?' He walked over to the window to have a look. 'Well, I might have known. It's that mischievous cat, Naughty Tortie! She always seems to know when I'm baking.' He banged on the window at her. 'Shoo!'

But Naughty Tortie was not going to go that easily. Why should Treacle have all that lovely food which found its way onto the floor? She jumped back onto the ground and slunk round the side of the house, waiting for her opportunity.

As Mr Pattacake was pouring boiling water onto the jellies, the doorbell rang. It was the lady whose little boy was having the party.

'Come in!' said Mr Pattacake.

'All that food for just ten children?' she said, coming into the kitchen and looking at the mountain of sandwiches and plates of fairy cakes.

'Ten?' said Mr Pattacake. 'But your letter said a hundred.'

She shook her head. 'Ten children will be difficult enough. The entertainer is ill and I can't get anyone else at such short notice. I don't know what we are going to do. I came to ask if you knew any party entertainers.'

Mr Pattacake didn't. Except for Treacle that is. Treacle had his little act, but that was best left as a secret for now. No one would believe it unless they saw it. All he could think about were the hundreds of sandwiches, the thousand mini sausages, and all the rest of the food. How he hated wasted food!

'I don't know what we're going to do, Mr Pattacake,' said Jack's mother. '*Please* try to think of something.'

When she had gone, Mr Pattacake went to read the letter again, but the ketchup had smudged the ink. He was *sure* it had said one hundred children. Had he been wearing his glasses when he read it?

'Now, Treacle,' he said, wiping his brow with a handkerchief and opening the window for some fresh air. 'What are we going to do with all this food?'

Treacle would have normally had the answer to that question, but right now he did not want to think about it. He had eaten too many bits of chocolate mouse. So instead he just lay on the floor in a patch of sunlight, his eyes half-closed, feeling slightly sick.

'You've eaten too much, haven't you?' Mr Pattacake said. 'Chocolate isn't good for cats. Now, where was I? Ah, I was making the jellies.'

As he stared at the giant jelly moulds, he had an idea.

After he'd put the popping corn in the pan to pop, he went out of the door and into his garage.

Lying against one wall was the new rigid pond liner which he was going to use to make a lovely pond in the garden when he had the time. It was a very big pond liner.

Mr Pattacake took off the plastic wrapping and smiled happily. His idea would at least solve one problem. He went back to his kitchen. While he was out in the garage, he had left Treacle in charge. That may not have been a good idea, although he knew Treacle had had enough to eat, so he would not steal any food.

However, he had forgotten about Naughty Tortie.

The tortoiseshell cat had seen her chance and sneaked in through the open window. Mr Pattacake looked at the mess with dismay. On the worktop the monkey tail sandwiches had been torn apart and all the chicken and cream cheese licked away, leaving bits of bread scattered everywhere. A carton of milk had been knocked over and was gently glug-glugging over the big plate of fairy cakes, which were turning to mush.

Mr Pattacake was speechless and his big chef's hat wobbled wildly.

'OH DRIBBLE !' he said. 'Treacle! Where are you?'

The big ginger cat crept out of a cupboard, where he'd been hiding. He looked ashamed of himself and could barely look Mr Pattacake in the eye.

But secretly, Mr Pattacake knew that Treacle was no match for Naughty Tortie, especially when he had eaten so much. Naughty Tortie, on the other hand, could be loving and purry when she wanted, yet turn into a wild animal when the mood took her.

The popping corn was now beginning to sizzle.

Mr Pattacake stepped carefully into the mess, but not carefully enough. His foot slipped on a splodge of cream cheese, and for a moment he slid across the kitchen floor like an ice skater, although not as gracefully.

Then, with a crash, he landed on the floor on his bottom. He narrowly missed Treacle, who had to move quickly, which was quite a struggle, especially after eating all that chocolate.

'Ouch!' said Mr Pattacake, struggling to his feet. 'This is not turning out to be a very good day.'

So as well as having to clean up the mess and make the sandwiches and fairy cakes all over again, (although not as many this time round), Mr Pattacake also created his **BIG IDEA**.

The popping corn was getting hotter, and jiggling in the pan…

There was still the problem of too much food, and Treacle couldn't come up with a single suggestion as to what to do with it, so in the end Mr Pattacake thought of a plan himself, and phoned Jack's mum to explain.

He had just put down the phone, when there was a loud **POP** and then a **CRACK.** Mr Pattacake jumped, and Treacle screeched, shooting out of the cat-flap like a rocket.

They had both forgotten about the corn.

POP! CRACK!

BANG!

The newly-made chocolate mice jumped too.

The mice that had already set landed back on the worktop and broke, but those which were only half set stuck to the ceiling, drooped, and fell onto the floor in chocolaty splodges.

'**OH DRIBBLE !**' exclaimed Mr Pattacake. He did another silly dance, but this time out of annoyance. More chocolate mice would have to be made.

At two o'clock he loaded all the food into the van as well as the **BIG IDEA** and the birthday cake (including wheels). He then drove slowly through the town with his window open.

'Come to a children's party in the park!' he shouted. 'Free food and drink.'

Treacle was feeling much better, so he sat on the roof, doing what he did best (besides eating). He played a jolly tune on his lute, plucking its many strings delicately.

Whether it was Mr Pattacake's shouting or Treacle playing the lute, the children and their parents soon began to follow the van, running and skipping with excitement, just like when the Pied Piper led all the children out of Hamlyn.

When they reached the park, Mr Pattacake opened the doors of the van and the children crowded round.

'Can I help, Mr Pattacake?' It was Jack, whose birthday it was.

'Mr Pattacake's party in the park,' said Daisy, giggling as she reached out for a bowl of popcorn and took it to a park table.

'With pink popcorn and pizzas,' said Jack, coming back for another plate.

'And me with a black and blue bruised bum,' said Mr Pattacake, recalling how he'd slipped and fallen, and nearly doing a replay in the process.

When it was all laid out, the children ate and drank and played while the mums and dads sat on a bench or on the grass and had a rest. Mr Pattacake just leaned against a tree. (You know why he didn't sit down, don't you?)

Suddenly there was a commotion.

'Mr Pattacake!' Daisy came running towards him. 'Some big girls are stealing our food.'

'They can have some too, Daisy.'

'No, but they're putting packets of crisps in their bags,' Daisy panted, partly from running and partly from outrage.

'And they're throwing popcorn all over the place.'

Mr Pattacake stood up to his full height and adjusted his big chef's hat. Stealing he did not like, but wasted food he absolutely *loathed*. He strode down to where two older girls were stuffing things in a bag, surrounded by the younger children, who were all shouting.

'What's going on?' Mr Pattacake fumed as his big chef's hat wobbled with disapproval. When the girls turned and saw him, they laughed.

'What are you going to do about it?' one of them said. 'It's a free party.'

'You're welcome to eat the food here,' said Mr Pattacake, 'but you're not welcome to take it away or throw it about.'

In response, the other girl picked up a handful of popcorn from a bowl and threw it at him.

The younger children gasped, and there was silence as they watched Mr Pattacake's hat wobble violently, as if he were going to explode. Then some of them glared at the girl standing next to Jack.

'That's your sister, Sara. Why don't you say something?'

'Yes, tell her to stop spoiling our party.'

'She won't take any notice of me,' said Sara.

'Isn't your mum here?' asked Jack.

Sara shook her head. 'No, I came with Daisy's mum.'

The older girls smirked at Mr Pattacake and continued filling their bags.

Suddenly, there was a terrible yowl, which made everyone jump and back away from the source of the noise.

Treacle's fur was standing on end and his tail was fluffed up to twice its normal size. His back was arched and his teeth bared. He yowled again and raised a paw, claws extended. Then he growled and spat and hissed.

The two girls jumped back, eyes wide with fear. Then they dropped their bags and ran, and all the children cheered. They looked down at Treacle, who was now back to his normal size and purring loudly, a big cat's smile on his face.

'Treacle! Treacle!' Jack chanted. Everyone else joined in as well. Mr Pattacake secretly hoped they would stop before Treacle became impossible to live with. He would expect all sorts of extra treats for being the hero of the hour.

Everyone cleared up the leftovers and took them to Mr Pattacake's van. Just before four o'clock, the mums and dads gathered up their tired children and went home, all except for the nine children who had been invited to Jack's party. *They* still had the best part to come. The birthday cake!

While the children went back to Jack's house in their parents' cars, Mr Pattacake and Treacle set off in the van.

Jack's house was on a hill, so Mr Pattacake made sure the handbrake was on. He didn't want his van rolling away.

Ten children burst out of the door and ran to meet them.

Ten pairs of eyes watched as he opened the van doors. What was Jack's cake going to be like? They knew that Mr Pattacake had made fairy castles and spaceships, and dragons and witches before. His cakes were legendary.

The **BIG IDEA** was right at the back and out of sight.

Suddenly, there was a rumbling noise and a clatter. Then something rolled out of the van, landed with a crash on the road, and set off rolling down the hill on its real wheels.

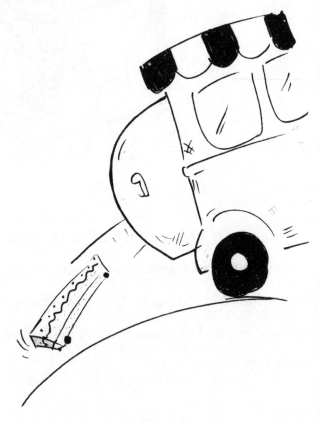

It was Jack's cake, shaped like a skateboard.

It took everyone by surprise. They all gasped and watched as it began to roll down the hill. Everyone seemed frozen in shock, and not one of them thought to grab it before it picked up speed.

'My cake!' shouted Jack.

He and Daisy set off after it, followed by the other children. Mr Pattacake was rooted to the spot, his heart thumping. He could only watch as it sped away, knowing he couldn't run fast enough to catch the cake. A cake on wheels (real ones) was very fast indeed.

All that work for nothing. And poor Jack now had no cake, because at the bottom of the hill was the main road. Mr Pattacake felt miserable. He hated it when things went wrong, and they often did.

The children would be smart enough to stop at the main road, but the cake wouldn't. It knew nothing about the dangers of traffic, and besides, it didn't have any brakes.

But Mr Pattacake couldn't just stand there. Even though he had no chance of catching the cake, he had to do something. So he set off after it, behind Jack and his nine friends.

They all hurtled down the hill.

Treacle didn't run. He decided that it was a waste of time and energy, although he could probably run faster than any of them. But it was futile. There was no chance of catching up with a cake which had had a head start.

As he watched the commotion, he saw something run out in front of the cake.

It was Naughty Tortie!

'Watch out, Naughty Tortie!' panted Mr Pattacake. Although the cat was a nuisance, he still didn't want her to get run over by a runaway cake.

Even Treacle was worried. His head was craned forward and he didn't move a whisker.

But Naughty Tortie just stood bravely in the middle of the road right in the path of the cake.

The children stopped, gasping for breath, and watched. Mr Pattacake staggered to a stop. He really needed to save his energy for later.

As the cake hurtled towards her, Naughty Tortie just put out her paw, and stopped the cake in its tracks. Then she stood there, her paw still resting on the skateboard cake.

Naughty Tortie stared at Mr Pattacake and he stared back. He had been around cats long enough to know exactly what they were thinking. The tortoiseshell cat was not going to let them have the cake unless she was invited to the party.

'What do you think, Jack?' said Mr Pattacake.
'Shall we invite her to your party? That's the only way
she will let us have the cake.'

Jack was looking at the cake with disbelief. The journey down the hill had not spoilt it one bit. It was such a realistic cake he could have almost put his foot on it and whizzed down the rest of the hill. But if Naughty Tortie lifted her paw, the cake would hurtle into the traffic on the main road and make an awful mess.

'Of course,' he said. 'Come on, everyone, let's have some cake. You too, Naughty Tortie.'

Mr Pattacake carefully picked up the cake, while Naughty Tortie turned on her purriest, smoochiest charm as she followed the little crowd of children back to Jack's house.

Mr Pattacake set the table and put out the paper hats and blew up the balloons, which were Jack's favourite colours of blue and yellow, and just a few purple ones too. There were party poppers and paper plates with **Happy Birthday** written on them, as well as plastic cups for the drinks.

Then Mr Pattacake placed the cake onto the table and wedged something against the real wheels, while Jack's mum fetched a knife.

He left the **BIG IDEA** in the van.

Jack carefully cut his cake in half and then his mum cut it into small pieces, and handed them out on the paper plates.

She was looking worried again. 'I'm really no good at party games,' she said. 'I do wish we had the entertainer.'

Mr Pattacake just smiled and went out to his van.

The children played pass the parcel and musical chairs and pin the tail on the donkey.

When their cake had settled, Mr Pattacake said. 'I have a surprise. Come and see.'

Everyone followed him to the back door and ran outside.

On the lawn, stood a giant bouncy castle. It wobbled gently as Treacle sat on top, washing his paw.

Jack ran to it and stared. 'It's made of jelly!' he said, poking at it. 'A giant jelly bouncy castle!'

'I made it with extra strong jelly crystals,' said Mr Pattacake. 'So I'll be the first one to test it out.'

He took off his shoes and climbed onto the jelly, which wobbled even more and CATapulted Treacle into the air. He landed on his feet on the lawn, looking surprised whilst the children giggled.

Mr Pattacake wobbled. Then just as it seemed he would fall off, he began to bounce, leaping into the air, doing somersaults and handstands. He did pike jumps and front and back drops. His big chef's hat flew off when he did a half twist, and it spun through the air and landed in the pond. He was enjoying himself so much that he forgot about his bruises.

'And now,' said Mr Pattacake, stopping for a moment to get all the children's attention. 'I'm going to do a special trick called a *barani*. Please don't try this unless you are really good at trampolining.'

He began to bounce again, higher and higher. Then he bounced up, began a somersault and twisted in the air, landing again on his feet.

Everyone cheered.

Mr Pattacake bowed and climbed down off the jelly. He was out of breath and wiped his forehead with a hanky.

'Can I have a go, please?' asked Jack.

'Of course. You are the birthday boy, Jack,' said Mr Pattacake with a chuckle.

Jack carefully climbed onto the jelly and began jumping up and down.

'It's fantastic!' he said, beaming.

Soon everyone was having a go, and there were squeals and giggles as they all bounced up and down.

Mr Pattacake smiled with satisfaction. 'My pond liner made a good jelly mould.'

'Thank you, Mr Pattacake,' said Jack's mum. 'Not only did you make the food, but you sorted out the entertainment too!'

'And here's your hat, Mr Pattacake,' said Jack, who had fished it out of the pond. It was covered with green, slimy pond weed so Mr Pattacake took it carefully between two fingers and pulled a disgusted face. 'I don't think I'll wear it until it's been washed,' he said.

And as the children jumped and laughed, Treacle gently strummed his lute under the shade of an apple tree, while Naughty Tortie lay on her back in a patch of warm sunlight, cleaning her claws.